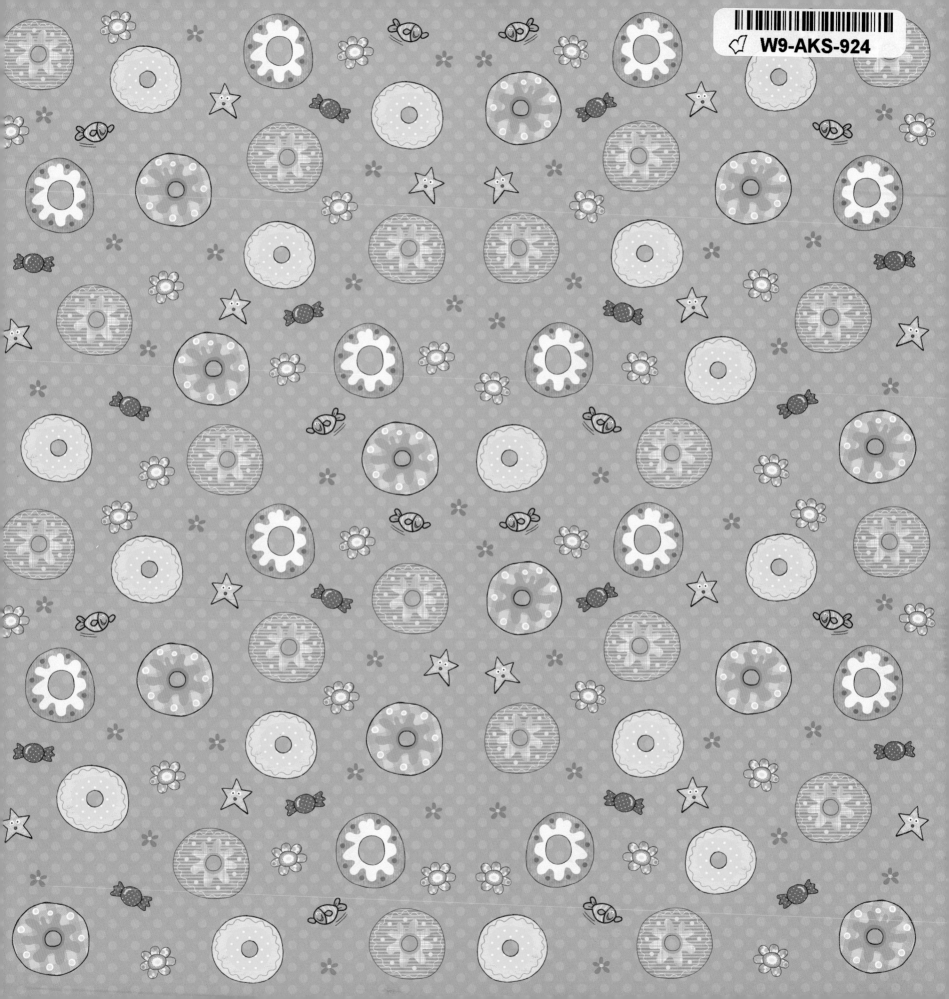

This book belongs to

....

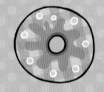

Written by Tim Bugbird
Illustrated by Lara Ede
Designed by Annie Simpson

Daisy the Donut Fairy

Tim Bugbird · Lara Ede

make
believe
ideas

Once upon an island
in the **deep blue** sea,
lived a **mermaid** fairy family —
Daisy, Dolly, and Dee.

Days were filled with fun
as the fairies swam and flew,
but apart from making donuts,
there wasn't much to do!

Donut Island

Their fairy wands made every kind –
hundreds by the hour!
But the donut mountains grew and grew
'til there was no room in their tower.

So Daisy called a meeting of her fairy clan.
They put their heads together — what they needed was a plan!

Daisy, Dee, and Dolly thought hard for hours and hours.
Finding uses for the donuts used up all their fairy powers!

Wheels

The **first** idea was Dolly's —
it didn't work the way she **wished**:
the **wheels** looked

good enough to eat

but soon got very **squished**!

Earrings

This was Dee's **best** idea,
but she didn't think it through –
they were far **too big** to dangle,
and the $frosting$
stuck like glue!

Sunglasses

The **third** idea was **Daisy's**. At first it seemed quite good, but **glasses** made from **donuts** just don't work the way they should!

It was nothing
less than awful –
there was nothing
left to try.

At least that's what the fairies thought, until a pirate ship sailed by.

Pancake Pete was **all aboard**
with first mate Fearsome Fred,
but neither one could see the **rocks**
with the **pancakes** on their heads!

Overboard the pirates jumped

as their ship began to sink.

Uh-oh!

Crunch!

Peering through the window
and thinking very fast,
Daisy said, "I think we have
a use for these at last!"

Donut Island

She took some donuts from the pile and threw them to the boat.
The pirates jumped inside the rings –
they really helped them float!

The Pancake Pirates **bobbed** to shore,
their timbers all a-shiver.

Dee and Dolly felt quite scared,
and Daisy began to quiver.

But Pete said,
"Please don't worry!

We're really
not **that** bad,

and sailing *donut dinghies* was the most fun we've **ever** had!"

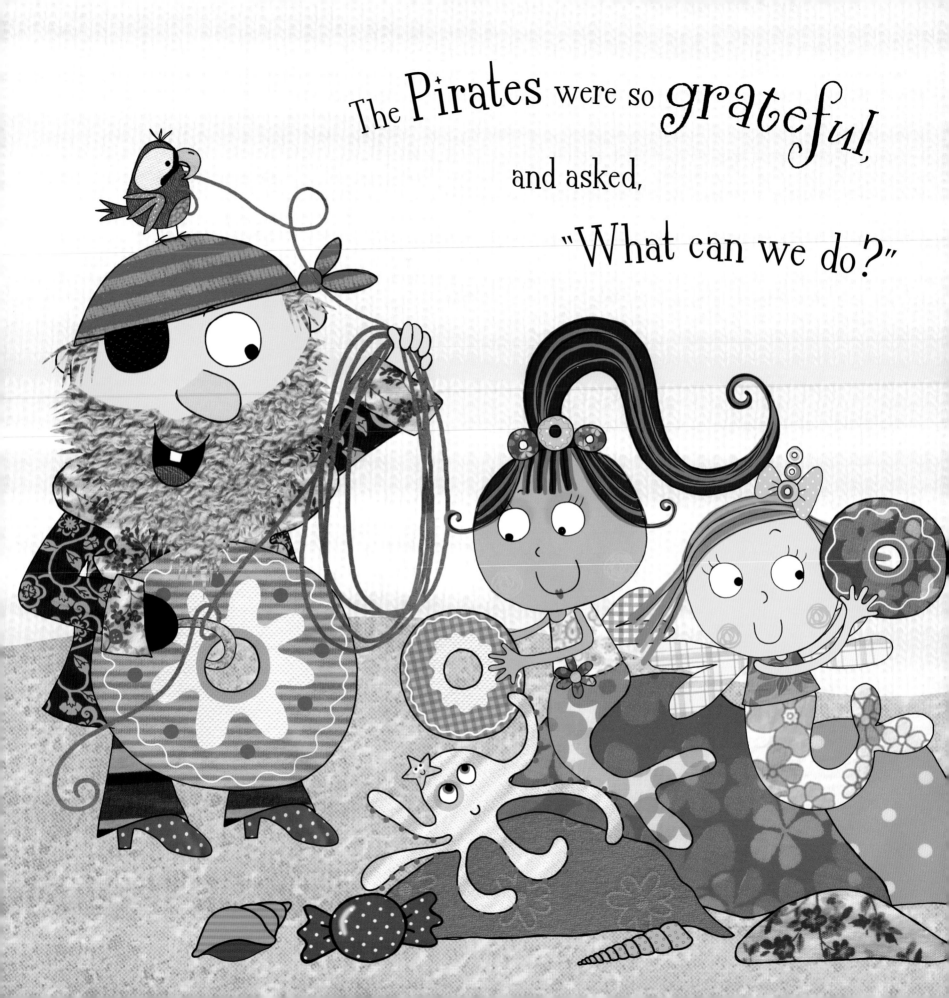

The Pirates were so grateful, and asked, "What can we do?"

Daisy said,
"There's a job for us
in sea search and rescue!"

So the fairies and the pirates learned how to work together, helping those in trouble at sea or lost in stormy weather.

Every day was an adventure,
hard work but full of fun,
and their donuts
had a use at last –
every single one!

So throwing donuts out to sea stopped the pirates from sinking,

and that's how Daisy saved the day, with true friends and quick thinking!

Dolly

Dee

Daisy

Pancake Pete

Fearsome Fred

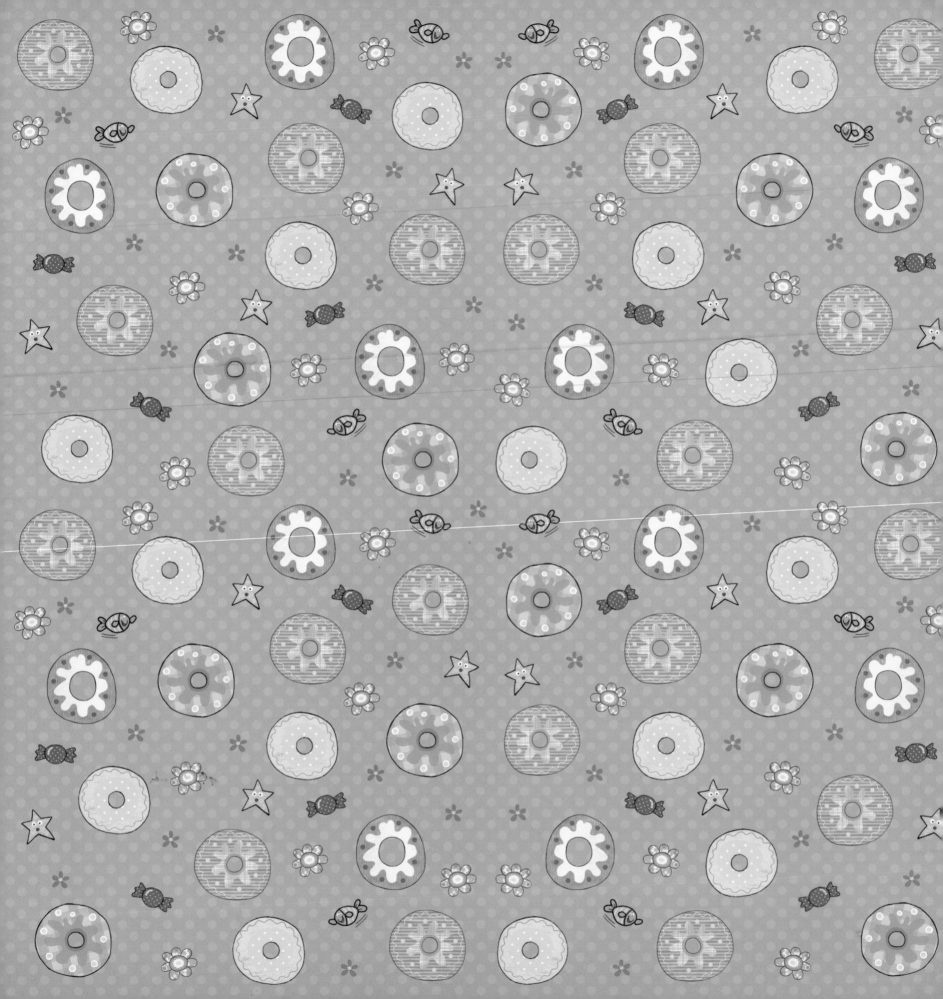